ADVENTURES AT TALL OAKS: NEW FRIENDS

By Elena Pavlova

Illustrations by Ingrid Magalinska

Text and illustrations copyright © 2004 by Elena Pavlova
Published by Read 2 Children
P.O. Box 4113, Warren, NJ 07059
For information, or to place an order, log onto:
www.read2children.com
First US Edition, August, 2004
Library of Congress: 2004093735
ISBN 0-9755839-0-5 Hardcover
Book design and layout by ArtVision
www.draw4kids.com
Printed in Hong Kong

To my grandfather. Your love is always with me.

CHAPTER 1

Where so many things happen

The sky gets very sick

If you count ten very big steps, ten regular steps, and eight and a half baby steps from the place where Itsy Brook makes a slight bend; turn quickly and hop five times on your left leg and then five on your right; make a few really high jumps and twirl around twice; you will find yourself at a nice street with not-so-big houses and tall, old oak trees. In one of those houses live two children, Denny and Maggie. There is absolutely nothing unusual about them, and though of course, they are very special to their family, they are just regular kids–like you. They like to play and do not like to clean up; they like to run around, but hate to fall down and scrape their knees; they are not very fond of oatmeal, but love to eat ice cream, candy, and cake.

The day when this whole story began started like any other, but later in the morning, when the children were watching their favorite show on TV, the sky seemed to have gotten under the weather: it frowned with all its clouds and grew dark, winced and gurgled as if it had a stomachache, and then broke out sneezing and coughing, which resulted in a strong wind brushing roughly through the treetops. Then, all of a sudden, a loud thunderclap shook the whole street and the house where Denny and Maggie lived. The children ran up to the window.

Ka-boom! went the thunder, and then the lightning, like a pair of sharp shiny scissors, tried to cut the sky into two pieces. Denny got his little brass horn out of his pocket and blew an alarm sound, and Maggie held her stuffed monkey Ginger tight to her chest.

Ka-boom! The thunder was so close now. Maggie got scared for one short minute–just for a fraction of it, of course, because though she was younger than her brother, she was a brave little girl, and never got frightened without a good reason. And there was one that time! Because before Maggie could reassure Ginger that they were all safe in the house, the lightning came down from the sky and right onto their street! Something crackled and then it became pretty quiet in the room and all the children could hear was the sound of heavy raindrops banging on the windowpane.

Electricity escapes!

"It looks like somewhere a tree got hit and took down electrical wires–we don't have any lights in the house," Mother said as she entered the room.

"No lights!" Maggie worried. "What will we do when it gets dark?"

"We will light the candles," Denny said. "Right?"

"Right, but meanwhile we will have to do without," Mother said, leaving the children's room.

"It's no big deal," Maggie said, still clutching her toy monkey. She peered out of the window. The raindrops were smaller now and the sky was beginning to clear up. "It is getting nice again; no need to worry," she calmed down Ginger.

"We can finish watching our show now," Denny said and blew his brass horn happily.

They switched the TV on and sat themselves comfortably on the floor when they realized that the TV wasn't showing any signs of life.

"What happened?" Maggie asked. "Why is the TV not working?"

Denny looked at his little sister.

"I think I know," he said with authority. "It is e-lec-tri-city. The TV can't work without it."

"But the storm is over," said Maggie.
"Why can't it get some?"

"Mommy said that the tree took the wires down.
Electricity lives in wires."

"And it ran away?"

"Looks like it."

"Oh," Maggie said, "then the repairmen will have to catch it and put it back."

"Yes," Denny agreed, "and that might take a long time to do."

"I know," Maggie nodded. "When you try to catch something, it always runs away from you. Just like the soap in the bathtub!"

"Let's find something to do while they're looking for it," Denny said and tooted his horn to encourage the search.

There is NOTHING TO DO AT ALL

And so they started to look. Denny looked and Maggie looked, and she even asked her stuffed toy monkey Ginger to look, but there was just *nothing to do at all!* So they went to their mother and said together, as if they had been practicing all their lives, "We are bored!"

"Oh," said Mother, "I see. How about lunch then?"

"Lunch!" the kids said. "Lunch sounds so good!" And, indeed, it never sounded better!

After lunch Mother read them a story, and then another one, and then sat down with them and together they made funny faces out of dry noodles and beans on paper plates. And then she said, "All right, children, I'd better start with dinner early tonight because we still don't have any power, and I don't want to be cooking in the dark. You go and play."

They nodded sadly and took off, but somehow there was still nothing to do! The sun was shining brightly now, and the sky didn't have any sign of illness anymore. The naughty electricity, however, was still running someplace but not in the wires that went to their TV. Denny and Maggie wandered around their room, looking sadly at all their toys.

They stared at the dark television screen and said magic words, hoping that something would appear on it, but as I already mentioned, they were just regular children without any special powers, and their magic words did not make any difference. They really tried hard to find something to do, but let's be honest here—what could they find to do if there was *nothing to do at all?*

So they went back to their mother and told her their sad story. Without electricity, they explained, there was *nothing to do at all* and they were still bored. Very, very bored. Somehow, this time Mother did not like the sound of it.

"It is impossible," she said. "I don't understand how two children can get bored when there are so many things to do."

But Denny and Maggie just stood there quietly and almost cried— this is how bored they were!

"OK," Mother said. "I know what happened to you! You got the Boring Bug!"

"The Boring Bug!" Maggie exclaimed. "Is it dangerous?"

"Very dangerous," Mother said, "but I know a good cure for it."

"What is it?" Denny asked.

"It's fresh air," Mother said. "Put on your shoes and your jackets and go explore our back yard."

"But Mommy!" said Denny.

"But Mommy!" said Maggie.

And not without a reason: they knew perfectly well that there was *nothing to do at all* in their back yard either.

"Don't 'But Mommy' me!" Mother said. "It's final." And she helped them with their clothes and shoes, put Denny's horn into his pocket, stuck Ginger under Maggie's arm, and propelled them through the back door.

"Open your eyes!" she said. "And your ears too! Use your imagination."

And with those words she closed the door, leaving Denny and Maggie standing on the back porch all alone.

CHAPTER 2

Where even more things happen

Fresh air does wonders

The children stood silently for a while. How unfair it was! They were the saddest, unluckiest children in the whole world!

Quietly and reluctantly they started walking to the farther end of the yard where the thicket grew so big it covered the white picket fence. Oh, the day was so pretty after the thunderstorm, the air smelled of spring, the sun gently touched their faces, but Maggie and Denny decided not to notice all that. They sat down on a big rock and started throwing pebbles into a puddle. The dirty water splashed on their clothes but they didn't care. It was not their fault that they were out in the yard and there was *nothing to do at all*, was it?

"It's so boring," Maggie said as she put her toy monkey onto a tree and tied its arms around a branch.

"I know," Denny agreed and tooted a very sad melody on his horn.

"Mommy said we should open our eyes and ears."

"That's really funny," Denny said. "They *are* open–otherwise we'd keep falling all the time, wouldn't we?"

"Or be deaf," Maggie added.

"Sure thing," Denny nodded.

"Mommy said there was something else we should try, but I don't remember what it was," Maggie said.

"Oh, we've tried everything. It is just one of those days. Nothing works."

"This is the most boring day ever," Maggie concluded with a sigh. "Poor, poor us!"

They sat on the rock shoulder to shoulder, their faces long, their eyes sad, doing absolutely nothing!

The ears start hearing and the eyes start seeing

"Look, there is the ferret," Maggie said and pointed idly at a slim dark animal that trotted in their direction, carrying something in his mouth. They knew that the ferret lived in the very back of the yard, and his hole was close to the fence. They had seen him a lot of times before, but there was something different about him on that day. The ferret always avoided the children and hid as fast as he could whenever he caught sight of them, but this time he was sauntering right toward them.

"What does he have in his mouth?" Denny asked.

"Oh, I think that's one of my old animal slippers," Maggie said. "Remember, I left them once somewhere in the yard, and they got all wet and muddy, and then—"

"No, Maggie, look! Really look! Open your eyes!" Denny said as he slipped off the rock and got down on his knees, pointing at the ferret.

"I have them open," Maggie argued, and to prove it she pulled her eyelids up high with her fingers.

"See," she said. "They are as open as they can be." She slid down by Denny's side and gasped.

"Oh! I can't believe my eyes!" she let her eyelids go as she clapped her hands in surprise.

The ferret put down the thing he had been carrying and stood on his hind legs, adjusting a red bandanna he was wearing around his neck.

"You'd better believe," he said and looked Maggie straight in the eye.

"I can't believe my ears!" Maggie cried. "The ferret . . . The ferret!"

"The ferret! The ferret!" the slender animal mocked her.

"Haven't you ever heard Ferret talk before? Well, well, what a surprise! Maybe you two should have your ears checked!"

The children knelt on all fours with their jaws almost touching the muddy ground: if by chance there were birds flying by, they could have easily gotten into their mouths and made nests in them.

13

"I can't believe it!" Maggie said again. "It is impossible! The ferret!"

"Maggie, what is that?" Denny whispered and pointed at the tiny bundle that Ferret had laid at his feet.

"A mouse!" Maggie exclaimed.

"Are you blind?" Ferret screamed.

"A baby elephant," Maggie murmured in disbelief.

"Yes," Ferret said with some poise.

"Oh no! Oh yes! " Denny drew a big breath. "What . . . what happened to it?" he stammered.

"Oh no!" Maggie cried. "It's so awful! The ferret was going to eat it!"

And in one instant she snatched the tiny creature and hid it in her hands.

"Why would you say that?" Ferret hollered, bouncing on his toes and tugging at his bandanna. "Imagine that! Silly nonsense! Eat him! Ridiculous! Where have you heard of ferrets eating elephants?" And he pierced Maggie with his two shiny blue eyes. The little girl blushed. It was true, she thought, she had not heard of ferrets eating elephants. Neither had she heard of ferrets reprimanding girls. She got very confused, blushed even more, and started looking like a ripe cherry. Ferret seemed to be quite happy with the effect of his words. Nevertheless he held the pause for another moment.

"I rescued them," he said at last. "They were floundering in the Itsy Brook and I saved their lives!"

"Their? How many elephants were there?" Denny asked.

"Two," Ferret said. "There were two of them. And I saved them both." And he proudly stuck out his chest.

"Where is the other one?" Maggie inquired.

"Well, why should I tell you? After all the nasty things you said about me?"

"Oh, please," Denny said. "Please tell us! Maggie did not mean to hurt your feelings. Tell him, Maggie."

"No, sir," Maggie said as politely as she could. "No, sir," she sighed and put the baby elephant down. "Here," she said. "I am very sorry." And her lower lip started to tremble a little.

"Huggy-buggy!" Ferret said and made a face. "I am Ferret, am I not?"

"You sure are," Denny agreed. "And I am Denny, and this is my sister, Maggie."

"I know," Ferret said. He pointed his chin at Maggie. "She can carry the baby elephant if she wants to." Maggie looked gratefully at Ferret, picked up the wet trembling creature, and cupped it gently in her hand. Maggie's lower lip was all right now and her eyes did not glisten suspiciously anymore.

"Huggy-buggy!" Ferret shrugged and then he paused for a moment. "I've made up my mind! You can go with me. Follow along and don't fall behind. I'll show you where all the action is."

CHAPTER 3

Where everybody meets for the first time

On the road to action

"Who would have imagined," Denny was saying to himself as they were scurrying behind Ferret, "who would have imagined that a ferret could talk just like a boy or a girl," when his thoughts were interrupted by someone's scream. They all stopped.

"Help!" somebody was yelling behind them.

"Oh, what now?" Ferret grouched and dashed back to the place where the screams were coming from. Denny and Maggie hardly had any time to move, when Ferret reappeared with the toy monkey.

"What happened?" Maggie asked.

"Who tied the poor animal to the tree?" Ferret inquired strictly.

"I did," Maggie said. "I always do, so she doesn't fall down."

"She can't fall down!" Ferret lost his temper again. "She is a monkey! Monkeys don't fall down! What is it with you people? Have you ever thought how she would *get* down?"

"Why would she want to *get* down?" Denny asked.

"Because I wanted to go with you!" Ginger burst out.

"Oh no!" Maggie cried. Still cupping

the baby elephant, she slumped down to the ground as if she had forgotten how to stand.

"Ginger?" Denny was about to tumble himself. "You can talk?"

"Of course, I can talk! Why wouldn't I?"

"But you never talked before!" Maggie said.

"Yes, I did!"

"Did not!" the children said together.

"Did too!" Ginger retorted. "I have always talked. It was you who never cared to listen!"

"Stop it!" Ferret interrupted. The tips of his bandanna were fluttering angrily in the spring wind. "The baby will freeze while you are bickering here! Everybody, quiet down and follow me!"

Denny helped Maggie up.

"Where are we going?" he asked.

"To Mrs. Cluck's," Ferret said smartly without turning his head.

"To where? To whose?" Maggie asked and was immediately concerned that Ferret would get upset again, so she added politely, "Sir."

"To Mrs. Cluck's," repeated Ferret. "Where else would I take you?" He glanced briefly at Maggie and added peacefully, "We're almost there."

The twins meet at Mrs. Cluck's

Denny followed Ferret and Maggie trotted behind, holding the tiny baby in her hands. Ginger stayed at the end of the procession and behaved like a real monkey: she jumped around, grabbed all the branches she could get hold of, and tried to swing on them. Moving in that fashion, they soon approached an old shed in the corner of the yard. Ferret plunged toward it and disappeared into thin air before everybody's eyes.

"I guess we're here!" Denny cried, almost running into the shed's peeling door at full speed.

"Watch out!" cried Maggie, who almost ran into Denny.

"Ouch!" screamed Ginger, who fell from a thin branch right onto the rickety porch.

Ferret instantly reappeared from under the door.

"What's the matter now?" he inquired caustically.

Denny examined the door: the handle had been torn off, and there was a big splintery hole in its place. He cautiously put his finger through it and tried to pull. The door screeched and would have fallen down on him if he hadn't propped it with his strong little shoulder.

"Bad design," Ferret grouched as he hurried to help Denny. Together they pulled the door aside, and everybody walked in.

A flow of warm evening light streamed in through the wide opening, and in the middle of the floor in a heap of golden straw Denny and Maggie saw a big black-and-white chicken who thrust her neck at them and spread her wings ominously.

"Cluck-cluck-cluck!" she started nervously.

"No need to worry, Mrs. Cluck," Ferret said. "They are with me."

The chicken folded her wings and nodded to the children without lifting herself from the nest.

"Mrs. Cluck," she said.

"Denny," Denny said politely and bowed his head, trying hard not to look too surprised.

"Maggie," Maggie whispered.

"Do you live nearby?" Mrs. Cluck asked, attempting to make some small talk.

"This is our . . . ," started Denny, "I mean, this yard . . . What I'm trying to say . . ."

"We live across the yard," Maggie said and waved behind her with her free hand, "Over there."

"I live with them," volunteered Ginger.

"I see," Mrs. Cluck said. "And what—"

But Ferret didn't let her finish.

"I am Ferret, am I not? I found the other baby!" he announced proudly.

"Oh, my!" Mrs. Cluck cried. "Where is it?"

"She has it," Ferret said, pointing at Maggie.

"Oh, dear! Give it to Mama! Put the darling into my nest! Where's my baby? Where's my precious chick?"

Maggie stood quietly for a moment. "Give it to her," Denny nudged his sister, but Maggie didn't move.

"It is not a chick," she said at last.

"Cluck-cluck! What do you mean?" fidgeted Mrs. Cluck.

"It is not a chick. It is a baby elephant," Maggie said with confidence.

"Don't you think she knows?" Ferret growled, tugging at his bandanna. "She just calls them that."

"Oh, nonsense!" Mrs. Cluck said. "Of course they are chicks! They just hatched."

"They are teeny elephants!" insisted Maggie.

Denny had never seen his amiable sister so determined.

"Ha-ha!" Mrs. Cluck cried. "Where have you seen elephants the size of a chick? They just look like elephants, but when they grow up they will make fine chickens! Now let the little one into the nest with its brother!" She lifted one of her wings and another tiny elephant peeped out and smiled at them.

"Oh, how sweet!" Maggie exclaimed without releasing the baby she was holding.

"Come to Mama!" Mrs. Cluck urged. "Cluck-cluck-cluck! Come to Mama!"

"You are not their mama!" Maggie protested.

"What is it? What is it?" Mrs. Cluck said, bewildered by the strange conversation. "Cluck-cluck-cluck! What are you saying?"

"You are not their mama!" Maggie repeated slowly.

"Maggie," Denny said, "how do you know she isn't? Maybe she is!"

"I am! I am!" Mrs. Cluck screamed.

"No, you're not!"

"Then who is?" the perplexed chicken asked.

"I am," Maggie said simply and lowered herself onto the floor next to the chicken.

"Denny," she said, "Denny and Ginger, put some straw around me. I'm nesting here. I am going to raise my children." And she brought the baby to her lips and kissed it gently on the forehead. It gurgled with delight and then caught glimpse of its twin's face, peeking from Mrs. Cluck's feathers.

"Brother! Brother!" it cried in a tiny voice.

Mrs. Cluck's feathers fluttered and the other baby ran up to Maggie and raised its morsel of a trunk.

"Don't you fear, sister. I am here!" he called in a brave voice.

"You are twins," Maggie marveled and let the baby boy climb into her hand, too.

"Cluck!" Mrs. Cluck said. When she got excited—and that happened very often, as we shall see—she often forgot how to talk and went back to chicken language.

"Cluck-cluck-cluck!" she repeated. "I've been robbed! I'm a mother without children! What will the other chickens say?"

Everybody is gathered now

"What other chickens?" Ferret asked and looked around.

"What other chickens?" two voices echoed from the doorway and two long shadows walked into the shed.

"Monsters!" Maggie whispered and closed her hands to cover her precious babies. But the two figures were not monsters. Attached to the shadows were a strange-looking chicken and a dark emerald frog. The frog had a long silky yellow scarf which he wore as a cape around his neck. The chicken had an eggshell top sitting on his head like a petite hat, while his wings and legs protruded from the shell's lower half.

"We have guests," the chicken said as he adjusted an eyeglasses frame perched on his beak. "Hello, my name is Gregg."

"Denny," Denny said and shook Gregg's wing.

"Maggie," Maggie smiled shyly at the chick. She could not shake hands because she didn't want to let go off her babies.

"Ginger," the monkey said.

"A pleasure," Gregg nodded. "I see you have already met my mother, haven't you?"

"Your mother?" Maggie asked.

"Let me introduce you," Gregg said. "My mother, Mrs. Cluck."

"My child is back!" Mrs. Cluck cried with relief. "At last! I was starting to get worried!" And as soon as she remembered that she was worried, she added, "Cluck-cluck!"

"No need to worry, Mother," Gregg began, but a long heavy sigh interrupted him. He turned around. Leaning on the doorway was the emerald frog who came along with him. He observed everybody sorrowfully.

"Greggy, you have totally forgotten about me," he said and dabbed his big brown eyes with his yellow cape.

"How selfish of me!" Gregg exclaimed. "Everybody, listen! This is my good friend, an unsurpassable poet and the best frog in the whole world. Please welcome Froger!"

The frog made an elegant jump, and his cape fluttered behind his back like a giant yellow sail. Totally ignoring Denny and Ginger, he landed on one knee before Maggie, took her hand, and kissed it.

"How sweet is your fist, all covered with mist!" he said in a deep silvery voice.

"Oh, it's not mist," Maggie said bashfully. "It's from holding my babies."

"Such a young mother!" Froger mused. "How old are your little ones?"

"They are just . . . ," Maggie stammered, "just from now," she said.

"Newlyborns!" Froger said. "Why, show them to us!"
Hesitantly Maggie unfolded her hands.

"Why, they are beautiful!" Froger cried.

"They are dwarf elephants," Gregg noted with surprise.

"Do not hesit*ants!* They are eleph*ants!*" Froger sang and made a gracious leap up and down.

"They are *my* babies!" Maggie said and hid her two

little treasures away from everybody's eyes.

"Huggy-buggy!" Ferret grumbled under his breath and slipped into a hole in the ground.

Ferret is a double hero

"Maggie, it is getting dark," Denny said.

"Yes," she said, "Denny is right. It's getting late. My babies and I need some rest. Everybody, please go home."

"We are home," Mrs. Cluck and Gregg said together.

"Oh!" Maggie said because there was nothing else she could think of saying, so she repeated, "Oh!"

"Maggie," Denny said, "*we* have to go home. Not them—*us!*"

"It's growing dark in our park," recited Froger.

"I can't go home!" Maggie said. "I am taking care of my children. I can't leave them alone at night."

"They won't be alone," Denny assured her.

"No, no, they won't!" Gregg said. "I love to read late, so I'll help Mother watch over them."

"The two of us will look after them while you're gone," Mrs. Cluck said happily.

Maggie's lips began to tremble.

"*I* am their mother," she insisted. "I can't leave."

"Of course you are their mother," Denny said. "It's just for a little while."

"I can be their aunt," Mrs. Cluck compromised, "and you can be their mother."

Maggie hesitated. "I don't know," she said at last and sighed.

"Though I am not educated as well on this subject as I am on all the others," Gregg said importantly, "I am positively sure that raising an elephant is a big job because it is a fairly large creature, you know. And perhaps they are not very huge at the moment; one can even say they are pretty small–chicken size, so to say–though of course for a chicken, I myself am fairly largely sized, but for elephants, that is—"

"They might grow big," Denny explained.

"Please, don't interrupt," Gregg pleaded. "Now I have lost my train of thought."

"It was a very long train," Denny said, "but I think I understand what you were saying." Denny was really good at math. "If raising one elephant is a big job," he continued, "raising two elephants is twice as big a job and you should use all the help you can get."

"I couldn't have said it any better!" Mrs. Cluck agreed. "Raising two chickens is not easy, but two elephants . . . Why, even an elephant can't do it alone!"

"And Maggie," Denny said, "you have to remember, if we don't show up at home Mommy will come looking for us and then . . ."

"Oh, no," Maggie said. "We cannot let that happen." She got up on her knees, made her way to Mrs. Cluck, and opened her hands.

"There, there, sweet babies," she murmured softly and gave each tiny face a gentle kiss, "Aunt Cluck will watch you while I'm gone. Have sweet dreams. Mama will be back in the morning." And she put them under Mrs. Cluck's warm wing.

"We have to go," Denny said.

"Yes," Maggie nodded and followed her brother toward the doorway. "No!" She stopped suddenly and turned around. "What will they eat?"

Just as she was saying this, the shed's floor shook and Mrs. Cluck jumped nervously in her nest.

"Cluck-cluck! An earthquake!"

Then one of the holes in the ground burst with sprays of dirt and out of it emerged Ferret, holding a white bowl with a blue rim half-filled with milk.

"You got me so clucked," Mrs. Cluck cried, but Ferret didn't listen.

"I am Ferret, am I not?" he asked proudly. "No one but me thought that the babies might get hungry!"

"Ferret," Froger said excitedly, "at first you saved the elephants' lives and then you saved them from starvation!"

"They weren't starving," Gregg remarked.

"They would have been shortly!" Ferret parried as he put the dish down on the floor and wiped his face with his bandanna.

"Ferret, you are a hero!" Froger cried.

"I will write an ode in your honor."

"A what?" Ferret asked.

"An ode," Froger said, "a poem in your honor!"

"Hmm . . . Could you read it here tomorrow, so that everybody would hear it?"

"Yes, I will work on it all night and it will be ready by sunrise!" Froger wrapped himself in his yellow cape and started walking toward the door, muttering something to himself.

"Adieu!" he said and then suddenly his eyes caught Maggie's.

"I will dream about you," he whispered. "That is, if I get any sleep."

"Huggy-buggy!" Ferret smirked and made a face.

"We have to go, too." Denny started dragging Maggie to the doorway.

"We'll be here first thing in the morning," Maggie said.

"Good night," Denny and Maggie said. They put the door back in its place and hurried back home.

"Toot! Toot! Don't come looking for us!" Denny blew his horn. "Toot! Toot! We're almost there!"

Was it for real?

The lights in the house were back on and dinner was waiting for them. Oh, they have never eaten so fast before! No playing with their vegetables! No attempts to rub the food back into their plates! They finished everything their mother gave them and thanked her for such a lovely meal.

When they were excused from the table, they did not beg to watch television; they brushed their teeth and washed their faces without any reminders, and put on their pajamas and jumped into their beds at such a speed that their mother started suspecting that perhaps somebody had taken her real son and daughter away and substituted them with look-alikes.

"Fresh air does wonders for kids," she said, switching off the lights. Then she remembered something.

"You didn't play with Samuel's bowl today, did you?" she asked. "I can't find it anywhere."

"No," Denny said. "We did not play with it." And of course he told the truth because the children never did play with the cat's bowl.

Later, when the lights were out Maggie sat up in her bed and stayed like that till Denny called out her name.

"Maggie, what's the matter?"

"I'm afraid to go to sleep. What if we wake up and it all turns to be a dream?"

"It won't."

"How do you know? "

"Remember that milk Ferret brought over?"

"Yes, what about it?"

"The bowl," Denny said, "remember the bowl?"

"The bowl?" Yes, of course, she remembered it! It was their cat Samuel's milk bowl Mother just inquired about: a white bowl with a blue rim. They never touched it and Mother said it disappeared! Ferret! It had to be Ferret! Then everything did happen! Everything was for real! Maggie smiled.

"I will get up very early tomorrow and bake cookies for everybody," she said. "Do you think they will like them?"

"They'll be begging for more," Denny said.

And they were both instantly asleep.

CHAPTER 4

Where two names and an ode
are sought and found

What's in a name?

"We forgot about the most important thing!" Maggie cried. The two babies just ate Maggie's delicious cookies, finished their milk that she had saved for them in her breakfast cup, and were chasing each other up one of her arms and down the other.

"What is it?" Mrs. Cluck sounded worried. "Oh, I am so forgetful! What did I forget this time?"

"We forgot to name the elephants!" Maggie exclaimed. "They cannot just be 'babies' all their lives, they have to have names!"

"That's right, that's right!" Ginger cried. "What should we call them?"

"We have to think," Maggie said. "Names are very important. A mis-named child will turn into a very unhappy grownup."

"Is that so?" Mrs. Cluck asked. "My son knew his name right after he hatched! First came the head, and then, a little later, the legs. And as soon as the head hatched, he said, 'I'm Gregg!' I, of course, had a different name in mind. But he would not respond to anything but 'Gregg', so I just gave up. His wings hatched later, but the rest of his body is still in the eggshell! Maybe it's because he has a wrong name! Cluck-cluck-cluck!"

"Don't worry, Mrs. Cluck. Gregg is a very intelligent chicken," Denny said. "He will all hatch when he is ready."

"I hope so. I don't mind having half a chicken, half an egg, of course, but I would prefer him to make a decision!"

"Maybe," said Maggie, who was only half-listening to Mrs. Cluck, "these babies know their names, too."

"It is easy to check," Denny said.

"How would you do that?" Ginger inquired with interest.

"I'll just ask," Denny said, and he let one of the babies climb onto his palm. "Hello," he greeted the baby, "my name is Denny, and what is yours?"

The tiny animal looked at him with curiosity. He thought for a moment.

"I don't know," he said frankly, and his face grew sad.

"It's all right," Denny said. "We'll find one for you." And he bent over to the other baby.

"And do you know your name?"

"No," the little one shook her head.

"So we have to find two names," Denny concluded.

"Where do we look?" Ginger asked. "Do we have to travel far? I love to travel!"

"No, we don't have to go anywhere," Denny said. "All we have to do is think."

"Think about what?"

"Think about what names will suit these babies," Maggie said.

"How would we know?"

"Well," Maggie pondered, "the names have to be nice, and the elephants have to like them."

One banana, two bananas

"Anybody who has any ideas, speak up!" Denny said.

"I have an idea!" Ginger cried. "Let's call them 'banana'!"

"It's not a name!" Denny protested.

"Sure is! It's the name of my favorite food!"

"Wouldn't that mean that the name is already taken?" Mrs. Cluck asked.

"Taken by whom?"

"Well, by that banana food you said you liked so much!"

"No big deal," Ginger said. "Banana won't mind sharing its name! Everybody else does."

"That's true," Mrs. Cluck agreed after some thinking. "We can call them 'banana'."

"Cluck-cluck-cluck!" she suddenly exclaimed. "Cluck-cluck-cluck! I totally forgot: there are two of them! Shouldn't their names be different? How shall we tell one from another? We'll call 'banana', and they both will come running."

"Aha!" Ginger cried. "That's actually pretty handy! If all the children had the same name, you wouldn't have to call each and every one of them! Just call out once, and they all come! And then you can just choose the one you need and let the rest go!"

Ginger got really excited.

"Just think! Say, you have to punish a child! You call: 'Banana!' They all show up, and then you can punish them all!"

"Why would you punish the others if they did nothing wrong?" Mrs. Cluck asked.

"You can punish them in advance," Ginger explained, "then you won't have to punish them the next time!"

"How smart!" Mrs. Cluck said.

"I know," Ginger agreed. "I don't understand why mothers haven't thought of it yet. It would save so much time!"

"*My* children," Maggie said sternly, "will not be called 'bananas'!"

"I thought you liked bananas."

"Oh, I do."

"Then what's the problem?"

"Banana is a food name, not a child's name. We need a child's name."

"Don't bananas have children?" Ginger asked. "I'm quite sure they do! And what do they call them, let me ask you? They call them 'bananas'! Because it is such a sweet name! So sweet, and smooth, and yellow. So tasty. Every time I hear it, I drool."

"Elephants are not bananas' children. They are elephants' children!" Maggie argued.

"And how do we know what elephants call their children? Maybe, just maybe, they call them bananas because it is such a delicious name!"

"Well, these children are mine, even though they are elephants."

"Can't be," Ginger said.

"Oh yes, it can," Denny disagreed. "I know a story about a boy who didn't have parents, and a pack of wolves raised him."

"I know it, too," Maggie said. "If wolves can raise a boy, why can't a girl raise elephants?"

"Cluck-cluck-cluck!" Mrs. Cluck shuddered. "So what did those, those . . . animals call the poor child?"

"They called him 'Mowgli'," Denny answered.

"What a strange name," Mrs. Cluck said. "Must be foreign."

"It meant 'little frog'. When they found him, he was just a baby and had no hair, so he reminded them of a frog."

"That was pretty smart," Maggie said. "Now, who do the baby elephants remind you of?"

"They look like little trains," said Mrs. Cluck, who once in her early childhood saw one.

Maggie had her hands clasped in front of her, and the two elephants ran in circles around her neck and along her arms, chasing each other. Their miniature feet went "top-top-top" and "tip-tip-tip," which tickled Maggie and made her giggle.

"I have a name," said Denny. "This one," he said and pointed at the boy whose feet were going "top-top-top," "will be 'Top' and the other," he pointed at the girl, "will be 'Tip'."

"Tip and Top! How wonderful!" Maggie cried. "Top!" she called. The boy elephant stopped and looked at her.

"Did you call me?" he asked.

"Tip!" Denny called.

"What?" said the baby girl elephant.

"It worked! It worked!" Maggie exclaimed. "Now we have babies with names!"

"Hooray!" cried Ginger, who was happy for the babies, even though her choice of name did not work out.

"Cluck-cluck-cluck!" said Mrs. Cluck, who was glad such a heavy burden was off her wings.

"Tip! Top!" Denny called and blew his horn to celebrate the moment. The newly named elephants smiled and stuck out their trunks, tooting together with the horn.

Froger breaks his promise

"We have to fetch Gregg and tell him the good news," Mrs. Cluck said. "He went to look for Ferret."

"Where is Ferret?" Denny asked.

"Ferret went to look for Froger. Froger promised to stop by in the morning with Ferret's . . . what's it called?"

"Ode," Denny remembered.

"Exactly! But Froger never showed up. So Ferret went to find him, and then he also disappeared. Then Gregg went to look for Ferret, and now they are all gone! Cluck-cluck-cluck!"

"Let's not panic and wait for them here," Denny suggested. "I'm sure they will show up any minute."

And he turned out to be right. No sooner had he said it, than Gregg walked in followed by Froger. Ferret, who looked pretty sulky, stepped in last.

Froger nodded to everybody. Then he saw Maggie and blushed.

"We have good news," Ginger volunteered happily. "We found names for the babies!"

"We called them Tip and Top," Maggie added.

"I have bad news," Ferret replied.

"What is the bad news?" Denny asked.

"The bad news is that Froger is a liar!"

"I certainly disagree!" Froger protested.

"Ha!" Ferret laughed. "Who cares? You broke your promise."

"I don't understand what you two are talking about," Denny said.

"I will explain," Gregg said as he adjusted his glasses. "Perhaps you all remember that Froger promised to write Ferret an ode."

"I remember!" Maggie exclaimed. "Tip, Top, quiet, children! Let's all hear the ode. I've never heard one before."

"You see, you see!" Ferret hollered, pulling hard at his bandanna. "She remembers! You broke your promise, you cheater!"

"I am not a cheater," Froger said in a trembling voice. "I am a poet. I tried hard to write a heroic ode in your honor, Ferret, but it wouldn't compose."

"What do you mean 'it wouldn't compose'?"

"The right words wouldn't come."

"You know plenty of words! Surely some of them would have been good enough for my ode."

"Maybe," Froger agreed without any enthusiasm. He looked down at his feet and drew several circles with one of them.

"This is terrible!" Ferret agonized. "Just terrible! I did all that hard work for nothing!"

"Don't say that," Maggie said, but Ferret wouldn't listen.

"Froger promised me an ode! You are all my witnesses! He said he'd work till dawn! Yes! And what did he do? He snored through the night!"

"I did not!"

"Oh, yes? You did, too!" And Ferret covered his head with his bandanna and made a loud snoring sound.

"I hardly slept at all," Froger said. "I had inspiration."

"In what?" Ginger asked.

"Inspiration."

"What's that?

"It is . . . ," Froger lifted his eyes to the ceiling, "it is a key that opens your heart so you can hear and see all the magic in the world."

"Couldn't you hear my ode?"

"I guess I could, but my inspiration made me hear something different."

"Like what?" Ferret asked from under his bandanna.

Froger blushed and didn't answer.

"What did it make you hear?" Ferret pried. "At least, I have a right to know! I am the one who is odeless here!"

"I gather you are right," succumbed Froger. "Fine, I will tell you, Ferret. I will tell all of you." And he adjusted his cape.

"Yes," Ferret said. "We are waiting."

"I wrote a love poem," Froger said humbly.

Ferret was quiet for a minute. Then he freed his head from the bandanna.

"Huggy-buggy! A love poem? For me? Well, all right, I'll take it!" He shrugged and made a face.

"It's not for you," Froger said.

"Not for me? But /am the hero!"

"I know."

"Who is it for then?"

"It's for . . . ," Froger stumbled, "it's for Maggie."

"For Maggie?" Ferret could hardly believe his ears. "But she didn't do anything! Why for her?"

"It was my inspiration," Froger said. "It doesn't take orders."

"If I meet your inspiration, I'll have a good short talk with it," Ferret said and gave his bandanna a strong tug.

"A poem for me?" Maggie exclaimed. "Why, how interesting! Nobody has ever written a poem for me before!"

"Would you like to hear it?" Froger offered eagerly.

"Why, of course! We all would," Maggie smiled and looked around. Everybody nodded, except Ferret, who still couldn't believe such treachery could be unfolding right before his eyes. Froger cleared his throat, spread his cape behind him, and started his declamation:

> *Oh, Maggie, Maggie, Margaret!*
> *Your eyes are blue, your lips are red!*
> *I'll serve you like a faithful dog!*
> *Oh, how I wish you were a frog!*

"Huggy-buggy, yuck-yuck-yuck!" Ferret cried. "Thank goodness, this is not for me!"

"Oh, Froger!" Maggie exclaimed happily. "It's just wonderful!"

Froger melted into a big happy smile. "You like it? Really?"

"I love it!"

"I'm glad," Froger sighed with relief. Then he turned to Ferret.

"I'm sorry, my friend, but don't despair. Your ode will come to me one day."

Ferret was pensive for a moment.

"Are you telling me one day it will just show up?"

"It might."

"Froger," Ferret said after another moment of thought, "when my ode comes to you, will it be anything like Maggie's poem?"

"I really don't know. It might. Why?"

"You know what? Don't look for it too hard. They're too . . . too huggy-buggy. And I am Ferret, am I not? I just don't think poems are right for me."

Ferret gets more than an ode

"Maybe," Denny suggested, "Ferret would like a speech!"

"A speech is when you speak?" Ginger asked.

"Exactly."

"Good idea," Gregg said. "So good, it could have been mine!"

"And what would you speak about?" Ferret asked.

"I would say some nice words about you, Ferret."

Ferret's blue eyes lit up and twinkled.

"I think I might like it," he said, trying hard not to look too interested.

"All right, then," Denny turned over a rusty bucket, got up on it, and blew his horn vigorously.

"Ladies and gentlemen!" he began solemnly. He knew that all the speeches started like that. Then he continued, "Today we shall say very nice things about our friend Ferret, a real hero and a very brave one, too! He risked his life and got all wet, which is no fun at all, because it's still pretty chilly outside . . ."

"He could have clucked a cold!" Mrs. Cluck worried.

"Or drowned!" Gregg said.

"Yes, he could have," Denny agreed. "It was very dangerous, indeed! Our hero saved two baby elephants from drowning in the deepest of all rivers!"

"Two, not just one," Ferret added.

"Yes, I said 'two'."

"I just wanted to make sure everybody heard how many."

"We heard, we know," everybody said.

"Let's clap our hands for brave Ferret!"

They all clapped. Ferret bowed to his gallery, trotted up to Denny, and whispered something into his ear.

"Of course, though we have to return Samuel's dish. Mommy has been looking for it all over the place," Denny whispered back to him and then again faced the audience.

"We also should not forget that Ferret brought some milk to feed the babies!"

"They could have starved! Cluck-cluck-cluck!"

"He also rescued me from the tree!" Ginger remembered.

"Well, what else can I say? Ferret is a hero all the way around, and we are all very proud of him!" Denny blew his horn, which marked the end of his speech.

Everybody clapped again. Ferret looked around and bowed his head.

"I am Ferret, am I not?" he asked with a happy smile. "That was just great! It feels so good when everybody says nice things about you. No offense, Froger, but I like the speech much better than a poem!"

"I understand," Froger replied. All of a sudden, he spread his limber arms and sang in a strong deep voice:

39

Ferret's so brave!
He fought with the wave!
He got all wet,
But he didn't fret!
He saved the day,
Hurrah–Hurray!

What was that?" Ferret asked. "It sounded great, too!"

"I think that was your ode," Gregg said.

Froger nodded.

"So you found it!" Ferret cried.

Froger nodded again.

"Today is the best day of my life!" Ferret hugged Froger first and then started hopping around, hugging everybody else and singing:

I saved the day,
Hurrah–Hurray!

Trying hard not to fall through the myriad of holes Ferret had dug in the floor, bumping into old long discarded things and into each other, everybody joined in the fun with Ferret and the newly named Tip and Top, and the day went as fast as only a good day can go.

CHAPTER 5

Where a tree turns into a house

The shed shrinks!

In the morning Denny pulled aside the shed door for Maggie, who was carrying a whole dish of her freshly baked cookies. She was about to walk in when she realized that there was room for only one of her feet! "Will you look at this!" she exclaimed while balancing on one foot. And it sure was an interesting sight!

It turned out that Mrs. Cluck had her nest moved to the side, where the roof did not leak as much, and was flapping her wings, trying to discipline Tip and Top. The twins, oblivious to Mrs. Cluck, were playing "catch" with Ginger, who roared around like a blazing fire, trying to tag them. Sometimes all three of them trampled over Gregg's head, which stuck from an old stove where he was lying,

reading out loud to himself. Froger was sitting absent-mindedly in the middle of the floor under a trickle of water, muttering something to himself. Ferret was spraying wet dirt all around him as he dug ferociously right under Mrs. Cluck's nest, which was about to cave in.

Maggie's head started spinning, and she almost fell over.

"Are you stuck?" Denny asked her.

"There is no room for my other foot."

"What do you mean there is no room?" Denny tried to peek in. "What's going on there?"

"Ginger! Stop for a minute! I want to walk in!" Maggie begged.

"If I stop, I'll be 'it'!" Ginger cried. "Tell them to stop first!" And she leapt from one wall to another.

"Tip! Top! Stop! I want to get in!" Maggie clamored, but the two pint-size elephants were making more noise than a herd of fully grown ones and did not hear her. Luckily, Denny had his horn with him. He stuck his head into the shed and blew it with all his might. The hubbub subsided as everybody turned their heads toward the sonorous sound. It became so quiet, they could hear the water dropping on Froger's smooth shiny head.

"Cluck-cluck-cluck!" Mrs. Cluck worried. "Somebody, help! I have gone deaf!"

"You are not deaf, Mrs. Cluck," said Maggie, who finally found a spot for her other foot and squeezed herself into the shed, letting Denny step in behind her. "The noise has stopped."

Mrs. Cluck looked around. Ferret had dug a hole almost half the size of the floor and was sitting so deeply in it, only his ears and the tip of his nose showed. Tip and Top stopped their wild chase right on top of Gregg's book. Froger sat in a puddle with his eyes half-closed, and Ginger swayed mischievously from a loose beam on the ceiling.

Denny and Maggie stayed by the doorway, holding onto the plate of cookies, onto each other, and to the wall.

"Cluck-cluck-cluck," Mrs. Cluck started hoarsely. She tried to say something else, but the words escaped her, and she could only repeat herself, "Cluck-cluck-cluck."

"What is it?" Gregg asked. Mrs. Cluck finally found her vocabulary.

"The shed," she whispered.

"What about it?"

"The shed has gotten smaller! Cluck-cluck-cluck!"

They all looked around. Mrs. Cluck was right. The shed had shrunk quite a bit and couldn't fit everybody anymore.

A house for everybody

"Magic!" Ginger cried.

"No magic," Denny said. "The shed is just the same; there are just too many of us doing different things at the same time."

"But it is nice to have everybody here," Mrs. Cluck said.

"It's so jolly when everybody is around!" Ginger agreed.

"All are welcome!" Gregg chimed in, shaking Tip and Top off his book.

"We like to be together!" everybody started saying to each other. "It's so much fun!"

"I know what we have to do!" said Maggie, who finally made it into the middle of the shed and set the plate with the cookies on the old stove. "We need a bigger house!"

"Yes! A bigger house!" everybody cried, reaching for the cookies.

"Oh, cluck-cluck-cluck!" Mrs. Cluck worried. "We'll have to move! I'll have to pack my nest!"

"Don't worry, Mrs. Cluck," Denny said. "You won't have to pack your nest."

"But this is my favorite nest! I have to take it with me."

"You won't have to pack it because you won't have to move."

"I don't under—cluck!"

"You and Gregg will stay in the shed, and we will build a new house where we can do things all together," Denny explained.

"How romantic!" Froger exclaimed.

We shall all get together
In our new house,
Ignore the bad weather
And chase our mouse!

"We don't have a mouse," Ferret observed.

"We'll have to get one," Froger retorted with a smile. "What's a house without a mouse?"

"I would love to chase one."

"I don't want a mouse!" Ginger said. "I want a lot of branches in the house, so I could hang from them."

"We want a long core in door to run about," Tip and Top said.

"Corridor," Gregg corrected them. "You want a long corridor."

"This is what we want," the elephants agreed.

"As for myself, I would like an armchair to read in. Preferably by the window," Gregg said.

"How about we build a houseboat?" asked Froger, who lived in a pond.

"Better an underground home," suggested Ferret, who lived in a burrow.

"I have an idea!" Denny said.

"An idea! How wonderful!" Ginger exclaimed. "Where is it?"

"It's in my head right now," Denny said.

"Can you get it out, dear?" Mrs. Cluck asked.

"Nothing's easier!" Denny lifted his chin, blew his horn, and announced:

"We shall build a tree house!"

"That is a good idea," Gregg nodded. "So good, it could have been mine!"

"Let's grow a tree and in it build a house of our dreams," Froger suggested.

"Let's grow a banana tree! Then we'll always have food at home."

"A nut tree is better," Ferret said. "Then I won't have to run around gathering nuts."

"A hole tree!" Top said.

"What do you mean?" Maggie asked.

"We want a tree with a lot of holes in it, so that Top and I can play hide-and-seek," Tip explained.

"No, no," Froger said. "That won't work."

"Which one won't work?" Ginger asked. "I hope the banana tree will work."

"Neither will work," Gregg said. "Growing a tree takes a very long time."

"Gregg is right," Denny said. "We'll have to find a good one in the yard."

"I know the best tree for building our house!" Ginger cried. "See that huge one in the corner? Let's build the house on the very top, and then its roof will touch the sky!"

"We can't do that," Maggie said.

"Why not?"

"Because it will then be only your house, Ginger; no one else can climb that high, besides you and maybe Ferret."

"I don't want a house without friends!"

"We need a house where everybody can come and visit," Denny said. He blew his horn again. "Let's start our search."

Looking for the right tree

They all set out to find that very special tree. They caravanned around the yard, Denny in front, blowing his horn once in a while to scare away wild animals, just in case there were any; then Maggie, who had the twins in her arms, so that they would not get lost and no one would step on them during the trip; then Ferret, who circled each tree he encountered; then Froger, who looked more at the sky than at the trees and tripped quite often; then Mrs. Cluck, who said "cluck-cluck-cluck" all the way; then Gregg, who talked nonstop about what kind of trees usually grew in the back yard; and—above them all—Ginger, who hopped from one branch to another, crying, "This one is too tall! This one is too short! This one is too new! This one is too old!"

They had almost crisscrossed the whole yard and were heading back toward the shed when suddenly the *right tree* just jumped in front of them and stood quietly in all its glory. It happened so fast that the scouts did not quite understand whether they stumbled upon the tree, or the tree stumbled upon them.

"Oh!" gasped one half of the explorers.

"Ah!" gasped the other.

"We have been looking for it all over," Denny said, "and it was here by the shed all the time!"

"Funny, I don't remember seeing it before," Ferret murmured.

"It just jumped on us from nowhere," reflected Froger.

"It doesn't matter!" concluded Gregg, who did not believe that trees could jump.

"It doesn't," Denny agreed. "Whether we found it, or it found us—it's certainly *the right one!*"

They all walked around it, Ginger staying cautiously in the back: she liked to jump on trees, but she wasn't happy about trees that jumped. But the tree did not think of moving anywhere. It was an old apple tree, not too high, with a hollow at the bottom of its trunk and thick knotty limbs. There were some last year's apples scattered around it, pruned and withered.

Ginger tried one and puckered her mouth.

"Not good for eating!"

"They are pretty old," Maggie said. "Maybe the new ones will be much better."

Working together

"What will come first–the new house or the new apples?" Ginger asked.

"If we stop talking and get down to building," Denny said, "the new house will come first." He blew his horn to get everybody's attention: "It's time to build our house! Do what you can, and don't do what you can't!" With that advice, he blew his horn again, and everybody set to work.

What a busy sight it was! Denny and Maggie circled the tree; Ginger ran up and down the branches; Mrs. Cluck zigzagged back and forth, flapping her wings; Ferret disappeared and then re-appeared from various new holes; Froger picked wool; Tip and Top ran, colliding with each other; and everybody stumbled over Gregg, who sat in the middle of the traffic and observed it quietly through his glasses. Gradually, however, everybody figured out what they should be doing.

Denny and Maggie found an old wooden door half-buried in the ground. "Timber!" everybody cried as they set it on the lower limbs of the tree. It made the most wonderful floor, which Mrs. Cluck immediately swept and inspected for bugs. Froger brought cattails from his pond, and Ginger wove them cleverly through the branches, assembling quite a nice roof. Gregg fetched twigs; Mrs. Cluck shared some golden straw from her shed; Ferret began digging and soon disappeared in a hole to show up later all covered up with red clay. He ran around the rising house, touching everything with his soiled nose and his dirty paws, and before anyone could ask him to go and wash up, the whole house was covered with his prints.

"Oh, look what clucked!" Mrs. Cluck cried.

"No big deal!" Ferret said and tried to wipe off the dirt with his bandanna, but it was too small for such a big mess.

As it turned out, it was for the best because the sticky clay glued together all the parts of the house, and when Denny asked him to bring more, Ferret got very excited: for a change no one was upset about his digging; quite on the contrary–they *wanted* him to dig! In the end, Ferret dug so deep, Mrs. Cluck began worrying that at such a pace he would fall through the earth. But nothing like that happened of course. Everybody worked hard and did what they could, and didn't what they couldn't, which is a very sensible approach to doing anything, if you think about it.

Tip and Top get a home and an address

When the tree house was all done, Tip and Top showed up with an old mailbox.

"What could this be?" they inquired, putting it down.

"It's a mailbox," Gregg said. "Nice addition to the house. Every decent home should have a mailbox."

"Mailbox with a little wiggle," Ginger said.

"It's not a wiggle, it's number three," said Denny, who knew all the numbers.

"What does it mean?" Mrs. Cluck asked.

"It means our house is number three on street . . ."

"We don't have a street!" Froger cried.

"It's all right," Maggie calmed him. "See that small path that leads to the tree? It can be our street.

We just need a name for it."

"How do we find a name for a street?" asked Ginger, who by now had some experience with picking names.

"It's easy," Maggie said. "Just think of something that is close to our tree house and is pretty."

"Our mailbox is close," said Tip and Top.

"My pond is close," said Froger.

"My holes are close," said Ferret.

"Our shed is close," said Gregg and Mrs. Cluck.

"What are all those big trees called?" Ginger asked. "They are close and I found a very cozy hollow for me to live in one of them! I just wish they were banana trees," she added with a sigh because, of course, she loved bananas so much.

"Ginger, this is brilliant!" Denny cried. "These trees are oaks! We will call our street 'Tall Oaks'!"

"How romantic," Froger said in his deep voice.

"This is lovely," Maggie said. "Now we can all live here!"

"But I live in my pond," said Froger.

"I live in my burrow," said Ferret.

"I live in my new tree hole," said Ginger.

"We still live in the shed," said Mrs. Cluck and Gregg.

"We live in the mailbox!" cried Tip and Top.

"Cluck-cluck-cluck!" Mrs. Cluck protested nervously. "You cannot live in the mailbox!"

"But we are living in it already," Tip and Top giggled.

Ferret put a short log into one of his holes right by the tree house and attached the mailbox firmly to it. Tip and Top lay in it side by side with their trunks hanging out of the open door.

"It's a hole tree, just like we wanted," said Top.

"The log is the trunk, and the mailbox is the treetop," said Tip. "With a hole in it," she added happily.

"It's just perfect," Top smiled.

"But how will you get out?" Mrs. Cluck inquired.

"Oh, it's easy!" said Tip.

"It's a lot of fun!" said Top, and the twins slid down the open mailbox door to the ground and ran up to Mrs. Cluck.

"Don't worry, Aunt Cluck, we are very close to your shed," said Top.

"We'll come and visit all the time," promised Tip.

"Wait a minute!" Ginger cried. "If everybody has their own place now, why do we need the tree house?"

"We can meet here every morning and play together," Denny said.

"Yes! Yes!" Tip and Top squealed. "Let's play in the tree house because there is no room to play in our mailbox!"

"And our shed is too old to play in," said Gregg.

"And too small," added Mrs. Cluck.

"And my house is too high to reach," said Ginger.

"And my house is too deep to reach," said Ferret.

"And my house is too wet to play in," said Froger.

"So, it's decided," Denny blew his horn excitedly. "Our new tree house will be our play house!"

"Our fun place! And hop place! And meet place! And sing place!" everybody cried.

"I just composed a song!" Froger exclaimed. "Join me!"

And they all sang:

Our house is done! Oh, how much fun
We'll have here all together:
In cold or heat, in rain or sun,
Let's say, in any weather!
If you are lonely, do not fuss:
Stop by at dawn or late.
We built a house—hooray for us!
Oh, ain't we simply great!

CHAPTER 6

Where an ocean is crossed and the enemy is defeated

Why does one build a house?

"Does anyone know why one builds a house?" Denny asked. Everybody had been playing in the tree house for a while and was getting just a tad bored.

"It is obvious," Gregg said readily as he adjusted his glasses. "A house will provide shelter from bad weather and all kinds of danger."

"That's right," Denny agreed. "But why else?"

"You can have friends over," said Maggie.

"You can go visit your friends," said Ginger.

"You can play there," said Tip and Top.

"You can dig secret passages to your friends' homes," said Ferret.

"You can raise your children," said Mrs. Cluck.

"You can dream and sing in it," said Froger.

"Yes," Denny said, "but why else?"

"I don't see any other reason," said Gregg.

"We build a house so that we can travel!" Denny said.

"Build a house? To travel? Cluck-cluck-cluck! It doesn't make any sense!"

"I know what Denny means," Maggie said. "Sometimes you get bored at home, and then you go on a trip and meet with adventure. It's all exciting at first, but then you start missing your house, and when you come back it's the best place in the world."

"Exactly!" Denny cried.

"Very interesting," Gregg flipped through his book. "There is nothing about it in the encyclopedia, but I guess we can check out your theory by an experiment."

"What does he mean?" Ginger asked.

"He means we are going on a trip," Denny translated.

"All right!" Ginger yelled. "I just love trips! Can we go right now?"

"We'll go today," Denny promised, "but first we have to get ready for it."

"How do we do that?" Ferret asked.

"We should decide where we want to go," Gregg said.

"Wherever adventure is!" Ginger cried. "I just love adventure!"

"We learned that adventure is everywhere," Denny said. "We just have to keep our eyes and ears open."

"I can do that!" Ginger replied. "Can we go now?"

"No," Maggie said. "We need to pack some things for the trip."

"What kind of things?"

"Only bare necessities, something you can't travel without," Denny explained. "Let's get ready. Get what you need, and we'll meet here before the sun reaches the top of the apple tree."

Denny blew his horn, and everybody scattered in different directions: the children rushed to their house; Ginger climbed a nearby oak to her hollow; Mrs. Cluck and Gregg went to the shed; Tip and Top chased each other to their mailbox home; Ferret disappeared in a hole; and Froger hopped to his pond.

Bare necessities

When the sunrays touched the branches of the apple tree, Denny and Maggie ran up to the tree house. Denny was wearing a sailor's hat, and besides the horn, which he always carried in his pocket, he brought a water gun and an old map. Maggie had a big sweater tied around her waist, a Band-Aid in her pocket, a carton of orange juice, and a plastic bag with some freshly baked cookies. At the bottom of the tree they spotted Ferret, who stood by what looked like a pile of dirt and was studying a compass.

"We're ready," Maggie cried. "Where is everybody else?"

"They're in the tree house," Ferret said. "Where else would they be?"

"Then let's go join them," Denny said.

"We can't. Do you think I'd be standing out here in the wind if I could get in?"

The spring day was just splendid, and there was hardly any wind, but Denny and Maggie did not waste time pointing that out.

"Of course, we can get in! There is enough room for everybody now!" Denny cried. "Come on!" And he and Maggie hurried to the door.

If they weren't absolutely sure that there was only one tree house in their yard, they probably would have thought they had gotten to the wrong one. What used to be a cozy and a fairly big place to play in now resembled a warehouse that was about to burst. Denny and Maggie squeezed in sideways and didn't know whether they should laugh or cry. Judge for yourselves! Froger brought in an overstuffed pillow and lay on it, covered with his yellow cape, daydreaming and looking at something through a pair of worn-out binoculars. Mrs. Cluck was circling a monstrous wobbly heap consisting of an old sewing machine,

some faded curtains, and a bundle of straw.

Gregg was sitting on a stack of books so high his feet could not reach the floor. On his lap he had his encyclopedia; under one of his wings he held a flashlight, and a broken umbrella under the other. Tip and Top brought every little thing everybody gave them as a mailbox-warming gift, plus nine old pinecones they found in the yard, and a magnifying glass. Ginger was holding a long jumping rope, two rubber balls, numerous combs, some ribbons, and a blanket.

Maggie looked over her shoulder and realized that what they had taken to be a mound of dirt, dug by Ferret, was not dirt at all, but a pile comprised of an old shoe, two rusty dumbbells, a broken trowel, and several pieces of something they couldn't quite identify.

"What is all this?" she inquired.

"Our bare necessities," Ginger said.

"Things we cannot live without," Mrs. Cluck explained.

"How are you going to carry all this?" Denny cried.

"We have to carry it?" Ferret asked.

"Of course! We'll walk and climb mountains and cross rivers . . ."

"You mean we won't just be dreaming?" Froger asked from his pillow.

"You mean we won't just read about it in a book?" Gregg looked at them through his glasses.

"You mean we will have to leave?!" Mrs. Cluck cried.

"Of course!" Denny said. "It will be a real trip."

"But what if we forget to take something and then we find out we need it? What will we cluck-cluck-cluck?"

"We'll share," Maggie said.

"But what if you don't have what I need?" Mrs. Cluck insisted.

"Then we'll suffer," Denny said. "Adventurers always suffer."

"What does 'suffer' mean?" Ginger asked. She somehow did not like the sound of that word.

"It means you feel bad," Gregg explained.

The faces of the future travelers fell.

"Don't worry!" Maggie assured them. "We won't suffer a lot, maybe just a teensy-weensy bit–you won't even feel it!"

"I won't?" Ginger asked.

"No, it will be a very safe trip."

"As safe as we want it to be," Denny said and everybody relaxed. Then they did some thinking and took only what they really might need on the trip: Froger took his binoculars; Ferret his compass; Ginger took her jumping rope; Gregg his flashlight; Tip and Top took their magnifying glass; and only Mrs. Cluck couldn't be talked out of taking a small bunch of straw with her–she was convinced she would miss her nest too much otherwise.

Froger's pond goes beyond itself

"Adventure is everywhere!" Denny announced and blew his horn.

"We only have to keep our eyes open!" Maggie reminded everybody, and with that the adventurers approached Froger's pond, which was just big enough for Froger to live in.

"Adventure!" Denny cried.

"Where? Where?" asked Mrs. Cluck, who was still not very sure she wanted any.

"I want to see!" Ginger screamed.

"It's right here, in front of you," Denny said.

"My pond is our adventure?" Froger asked in disbelief.

"It will become our adventure because we shall cross it," Denny explained.

"What is there to cross? I can step over it," said Ginger.

"We can jump over it," boasted Top.

"If we run real fast, we could," agreed Tip.

"I can fly over it," Mrs. Cluck said proudly.

Ferret and Gregg just stood there: they were so disappointed they couldn't find words to express their frustration.

"Can't you all see?" Maggie asked. "Look closely at it! Open your eyes!"

Everybody peered at Froger's pond. Froger, Tip, and Top passed around their binoculars and the magnifying glass, and finally–who would believe it!–right in front of their eyes the little puddle of water started gurgling and twirling and spreading and deepening until it became as endless as an ocean.

"Cluck-cluck-cluck!" cried Mrs. Cluck, who became worried now. "I cannot swim!"

"You don't have to swim. We will build a raft," Denny said.

"A raft! A raft!" everybody cried, and they all started jumping around excitedly and then scattered in search of sticks and twigs. Ginger's jumping rope came in very handy when time came to tie all the timber together. The longest stick became a mast; Ferret's bandanna served as a flag; Froger's cape made a wonderful sail; and the longest branches became poles to steer the raft. They were all ready to begin their journey.

"I will be the captain!" Denny said, pointing at his sailor's cap.

"I will be the navigator!" decided Gregg. He borrowed Denny's map and Ferret's compass and started charting their course.

"I will steer the boat," Froger said.

"I will also steer the boat!" cried Ginger, who didn't quite know what that meant, but thought it might be fun to try.

"We will be the passengers," Tip and Top said together.

"I will be . . . cluck-cluck-cluck! I will be . . . cluck-cluck-cluck!" Mrs. Cluck was so nervous she couldn't find the right word. "I will be a chicken!" she blurted out at last. No one had a chance to say anything about it because Ferret, bursting with importance, announced:

"And I will kill the crocodiles!"

"What? Who? Cluck-cluck-cluck!" Mrs. Cluck nearly fainted.

"The crocodiles! The crocodiles! I will also fight the pirates!"

"We shall meet pirates?" Ginger asked with interest.

"Only if we want to meet them," Denny said.

"Who cares if we want to or not," Ferret argued, admiring his bandanna, fluttering at the top of the mast. "If we are in the ocean, there will be pirates." And he started pacing the raft with Denny's water gun.

"I will be everybody's mother," Maggie said last, and everybody was relieved because with all the uncertainties and dangers of adventure, having a mother on board was a very comforting thought.

The terrible storm

Mrs. Cluck was so afraid to sail, she decided to go back home, but while she was making up her mind about which way it was safer to step off, the raft left the shore as Froger and Ginger cleverly steered it into the open waters. The cool wind filled out the sail, and the raft cruised joyfully into the uncharted sea.

Tip and Top got so excited they couldn't stop running around trying to help everybody, and would have fallen overboard when they were trying to help Froger and Ginger—it's a good thing Maggie never let them out of her sight and was there just in time to catch them as they dropped down from the tops of the long poles. Then, all of a sudden, both twins fell asleep right in the middle of the raft. Maggie covered them with her sweater and started getting out cookies for lunch when Froger and Ginger noticed that it was getting harder and harder to steer the raft.

"A storm is coming!" Denny said.

On hearing this, Mrs. Cluck almost died.

"No need to worry," he calmed her down. "We'll do just fine."

Denny blew his horn and commanded his crew to pull in the steering poles, fold the sail, and hold on tight to the mast and to each other. Maggie picked up the elephants and tucked them under Mrs. Cluck's wings. The little ones were sleeping so soundly they never even stirred. Maggie sat down, hugging Mrs. Cluck, and Froger and Ginger held Maggie while grabbing on to the mast with their free hands. Ferret and Gregg grasped it on the other side and held a strong grip on Denny, who was standing at the front of the raft, unafraid of the growing waves and the strong wind.

The sky turned purple, and the rough water picked up the raft high up to the heavy thunderclouds and then dropped it down into the dark swirling ocean.

"Oooo! I will sink you-uuu!" the wind hissed, but the gang did not listen to him.

"Oooo! We will drench you!" the ominous clouds threatened, but the travelers did not look at them.

"Swish, swoosh! You'll never see the shore again!" the waves whooshed, but no one believed them.

"Troo-too-too!" Denny blew his horn. "Troo-too-too!"

"We need a song!" Maggie cried and looked at Froger.

"A song?" asked Mrs. Cluck.

"Why do we need one?" asked Ginger.

"We need a song to cheer us up!" Maggie said. "Froger, can you think of one?"

"A song to cheer us up is coming!" Froger declared readily and started singing:

> *The silly wind can blow,*
> *And threaten us, and hiss;*
> *We're not afraid. Oh yes? Oh no!*
> *We're stronger than it is!*
>
> *The silly clouds can glow,*
> *And frown at us, and grin;*
> *We're not afraid. Oh yes? Oh no!*
> *Together we shall win!*

The silly waves can grow
And make the sea a mess;
We're not afraid! Oh yes? Oh no!
We couldn't care much less!

Everybody was singing "Oh yes? Oh no!" so loudly, their voices pierced the clouds and reached the sun. When it heard such a courageous song, it peeked down at them, stopped the wind and the waves in their tracks, smiled at everybody, and relaxed in the middle of the sky.

Mrs. Cluck relaxed, too, spread out her wings, and Tip and Top rolled out looking like sweaty feathery chicks.

"What happened?" they asked.

"There was a storm," Mrs. Cluck explained.

"A terrible one," Ferret confirmed, "but we killed it!"

"Oh!" Top cried. "We missed so much fun! I want to kill a storm, too. Can we have it again?"

"I don't think so," Ginger said. "It's too boring to have two storms in a row. Let's have something else!"

Lurking dangers

Right then Ferret stood up on his tiptoes and peered at the horizon.

"What is there?" Mrs. Cluck asked nervously and looked in the same direction. "Are there some logs floating towards us?"

Denny looked through the binoculars and passed them to Ferret. Ferret squinted his eyes as he inspected the sea. Then his face stretched into a huge happy grin.

"Those are not logs, Mrs. Cluck," he said slowly and solemnly.

"What are they?"

"They are super-vicious, very hungry, mighty-bity crocodiles!"

"Oh yes!!!" the elephants screamed. "Adventure at last!"

"Oh no! Cluck-cluck-cluck!" Mrs. Cluck cried. "Too much adventure!" And she tried to tuck the twins under her wings again, but somehow this time no matter how hard she squeezed her wings, the sly babies kept falling out.

"Please, no panic on my ship!" Denny ordered politely. "Ferret!"

"Yes, Captain!"

"You know what to do!"

"Yes, Captain!" Ferret yelled at the top of his lungs and aimed his water gun at the approaching beasts. Now there was no doubt left as to who they were. The crocodiles were swimming up to the raft very fast, their long tails ruffling the waters, their vicious snouts moving hungrily, their numerous ugly teeth glistening in their open mouths.

"One, two, three! Three of them!" Ginger announced.

"No, Ginger, not three," said Denny, who knew how to count to a million. He continued: "Four, five! There are five of them!"

"Do you think they are all hungry?" Mrs. Cluck asked. She was worried, of course, not so much for herself, but for the silly babies who didn't even have an inkling of what was awaiting them.

"One hungrier than the other!" Ferret squealed with pleasure. He shook the water gun and aimed it at the fattest, biggest crocodile who was leading the pack. Squirt! And he hit the leader right in his yellow eye. The monster yelled in pain, shut the wounded eye, but continued swimming ahead, glaring wickedly at Ferret with his other one. Squirt! Ferret fired again and hit the glowing yellow target. The crocodile hollered and stopped. He could not see now where he was going. The others who were following him did not have enough time to slow down and ran into him at full speed, with the last crocodile landing on the very top of the whole pile.

"I reached land!" he thought at first, but the heavy pyramid began sinking and broke up, and the crocodiles popped out of the water, angry and humiliated. They circled the raft, but everybody was ready for them now. Denny and Maggie sent burning rays of sun at them through the magnifying glass; Ferret shot his gun; Gregg blinded them with his flashlight; Ginger and Froger poked them with the poles; Tip and Top sprayed them from their trunks; and Mrs. Cluck, who hated it when big bullies threatened little children, picked out the sharpest straws and hurled them at the crocodiles, aiming at their disgusting snouts.

"They are retreating!" Denny cried, blowing his horn in victory.

"Chickens!" Mrs. Cluck yelled and flapped her wings.

"We won! We won!" Tip and Top danced together.

Ferret didn't want to end shooting and continued blasting the fleeing crocodiles with his gun. He allowed himself to stop only when they disappeared out of sight.

"That will teach them!" he smiled contentedly.

"Those crocodiles were real cowards!" Mrs. Cluck said with disdain. "Imagine—the monster creatures were afraid of water squirts!"

"Gregg told us to add orange juice to the water," Tip and Top said. "It really stings if you get it in the eye!"

"How very clever!" Mrs. Cluck laughed and hugged the twins with her warm wings.

Home is best

Tip and Top suddenly realized how tired they were.

"I think I'm hungry," Tip said.

"The poor babies are hungry and thirsty!" Mrs. Cluck worried.

"Not thirsty, we drank a lot of juice while we squirted," Top explained.

"Well, hungry is a good enough reason for us to start back home," Mrs.

Cluck said and looked appealingly at Captain Denny.

"We haven't met the pirates yet," remembered Ferret.

"We'll leave them for next time," suggested Maggie.

"Course back home!" the captain commanded, and before they knew it, the ocean started shrinking back till it became a tiny puddle. Froger stepped into what used to be the middle of his pond, looking around in disbelief.

"My pond is all gone!" he sobbed. "What happened to it?"

"We probably splashed around a lot of water when we were traveling," Denny said. Froger reached for his yellow cape tied to the mast and dabbed his eyes with it.

"What shall I do?"

"Don't worry! Wait for us here!" Denny said, and together with his sister he hurried off someplace and came back in a flash with a bucket full of fresh water. They poured it carefully into the measly remains of Froger's pond and filled it right to the brim.

"Is this all right?" Maggie asked.

"How beautiful!" Froger exclaimed as he looked at his reflection in the water. He stepped in and shivered with delight.

"Good-bye, Froger," everybody said. "Thank you for letting us use your pond for our adventure!" They all gathered their belongings; Ferret tied his bandanna around his neck, and Maggie picked up Tip and Top. And they all went home, thinking that though their adventure was very, very good, getting back home felt the best.

CHAPTER 7

Where the old apple tree blooms and bears fruit

The best way to enjoy a morning

That morning started like many others: after everybody had assembled in the tree house, Ferret and Gregg began debating on how to spend the day, so that it would turn out to be as enjoyable as possible.

"I don't care what we do as long as we do not travel," announced Mrs. Cluck, who believed that one trip in a lifetime was more than enough.

"We only traveled on the ground," argued Ferret, who preferred underground activities to any others.

"Technically speaking," Gregg interrupted, "we did not travel by land. We traveled by sea. We were on a raft, remember?"

"Romantically speaking," Froger murmured with his eyes closed, "we could travel in our dreams."

Mrs. Cluck liked that idea.

"I agree to travel," she announced, "as long as I don't have to move."

"Oh, how boring!" Ginger cried. "We have to move! We'll get covered with moss if we don't!" And to make sure nothing like that happened to her, she quickly climbed up and down the wall.

"What are you clucking, I mean, saying, cluck-cluck-cluck?" Mrs. Cluck lifted her wings nervously and checked them for visible signs of moss or any other vegetation. There were none to be observed, but she flapped vigorously just to be on the safe side.

"That was not a scientific statement!" Gregg said to Ginger.

"Oh, yes?" Ginger cried. "How about you sit in one place for a week and then we see what happens!"

"How about you stop bouncing and rocking the house?" retorted Gregg, whose glasses kept slipping off his beak as he watched Ginger jump up and down.

"How about we all do something underground?" insisted Ferret.

"It's too dark underground; why can't we all just close your eyes and dream?" suggested Froger.

"Well, if we close our eyes it will be dark, won't it? So why don't we just go underground and keep our eyes open?"

And they went on and on, till everybody started speaking, hopping, and clucking at the same time.

"Underground!" demanded Ferret.

"Travel! Travel!" yelled Ginger.

"Dream!" begged Froger.

"We need a plan!" urged Gregg.

"Choo-choo!" tooted Tip and Top, who didn't have an opinion and didn't want to waste time arguing when they could be playing.

"Cluck-cluck-cluck!" Mrs. Cluck got very perplexed. "I don't understand what's going on!"

The apple tree comes to life

"What's going on?" echoed Denny and Maggie, who stepped into the tree house looking very excited. But no one heard them.

"Listen, everybody!" Denny tooted his horn to get attention. "Maggie and I saw something special!"

The clamor quieted down.

"Is it underground?" asked Ferret.

"No," Maggie smiled, "but it isn't on the ground either."

"Do we have to swim, cluck-cluck?"

"No," Denny said. "It's not on the water."

"Where is it?" asked Ginger.

"What is it?" asked Gregg.

"Let's go out; we'll show you."

Everybody hurried out of the tree house and stood still for a moment, observing the incredible magic: the old apple tree, usually dark and knotty, was all covered with clouds of fragrant white and pink flowers.

"When did it happen?" Mrs. Cluck asked. "I didn't see it when I came out earlier."

"I didn't either," Gregg said, peering hard through his glasses. "It must have happened while we were . . . er . . . talking about our . . . um . . . plans . . ."

"Is it snow?" Ginger asked. "Is it winter again?"

"Snow! Snow! It snowed on our apple tree!" cried Tip and Top, who had never seen snow before, but heard about it from Gregg. "We can go skiing!"

"We can't!" Maggie laughed.

"Then we can go skating!" the elephants continued enthusiastically.

"No, no, it's not snow!" Maggie explained. "We have snow in the winter, and it's spring now. Look around—see, the grass is green, and the flowers are blooming. The old apple tree, too, knows it's spring, so it started to blossom. Smell! Do you feel how sweet the air is?"

The twins diligently drew in the air with their trunks.

"Ahhh!" Froger suddenly breathed in too deeply and fainted right into Maggie's arms. Gregg waved his encyclopedia at him, but Froger remained as limp as a noodle. Ferret picked him up and shook him with all his might.

"Ahhh!" Froger sighed and opened his eyes. "How beautiful! I think I lost my breath!"

"Huggy-buggy!" Ferret grinned and made a face. "You lost your everything! I saved you!"

"Why, thank you," Froger said, rubbing his shoulders. "You didn't have to save me so brutally!"

"Huggy-buggy!" Ferret shrugged. He was about to say something else, but the resplendent tree made him stop. The fragrant air got into his head, too, and he swayed a little.

"It is . . . um . . . not too bad," he loosened his bandanna and stretched out on the ground under the long branches. Denny and Maggie sat down, too. Froger covered himself with his cape and lay down, leaning on his elbow. Mrs. Cluck landed down by Gregg; Tip and Top climbed onto Maggie's lap; and even Ginger stopped bouncing around and settled happily under the tree.

Where do bananas grow?

"Will it stay like this forever?" Tip and Top asked eagerly.

"Will it? Will it?" Ginger asked. "I hope it does. I really like it this way."

"I wouldn't give it more than a week," Gregg said.

"Only a week!" Ginger gasped. "And then it will die again!"

On hearing this, Tip and Top buried their heads in Maggie's lap and got ready to cry.

"Actually, quite the opposite," Gregg said as he examined the tree through his glasses. He was so proud he used two such important words in such a short phrase, he lost his train of thought.

"What does it mean?" Tip and Top lifted their wrinkled, ready-to-weep faces.

"Gregg is saying that the tree isn't going to die," Maggie hurried to explain. The twins' faces smoothed out. "When the blossoms are gone, the tree will have fruit."

"Fruit!" Tip and Top exclaimed.

"What kind of fruit?" Ginger asked.

"Apples," Gregg said. "It's only natural that an apple tree has apples."

"Just apples?"

"Of course," Gregg said. "What else would you expect from an apple tree?"

"Can it have bananas?"

"No way," Gregg replied. "For bananas you need a banana plant."

"Where can I find one?"

"Banana plants grow in Africa and other tropical places where it's very hot. They don't like it here–it gets too cold in the winter," said Gregg, who knew almost everything about anything.

"Bananas grow in Africa," Ginger repeated slowly. "If I hop from one big tree to another, will I get there?"

"Never!" Gregg said. "That is impossible!"

Ginger's face became so sad that Denny hurried to cheer her up.

"Don't say 'never', Gregg! Anything is possible when one really wants it. Africa is pretty far away, though," he said to Ginger. "You will have to do a lot of tree hopping and by the time you get there you will probably be an old tired monkey."

"An old monkey?" Ginger thought for a short moment. "That's too long a way for a banana!"

"I'm afraid it is," Denny agreed.

What grows on an apple tree?

"But isn't there any other way?" asked Ginger, who was just dying to have a banana.

"How about we just dream about what we want the tree to grow for us!" Denny suggested.

"Yes, let's all dream!" Froger said excitedly.

"How do we do that?" asked Gregg.

"We just close our eyes and say what we want the tree to grow."

"And then?" asked Ginger.

"And then whatever we wish for will grow on the tree!" said Maggie.

"Yes! Let's do that!" yelled Ginger, who couldn't contain herself and started bouncing again.

"I might try it, too," Mrs. Cluck said cautiously.

"That will never work!" Gregg predicted.

"Greggy, why do you have to be such a party pooper today?" asked Froger. "It won't hurt to try. I actually think I know a way to make it work."

"What is it?" asked Ferret, who also liked the idea, though he did not admit it.

"It's a magic chant!"

"Tell us!" Ginger begged. "Please! Tell us fast!"

Froger closed his eyes and stretched out his arms out toward the tree:

The magic wind goes swash and swish,
The apple tree grows what I wish!

"Yes! Yes!" Ginger cried and looked at the tree. "Did you wish for a banana? Where is it?"

"I did not wish for a banana!" Froger said. "Banana is your wish!"

"What did you wish for, then?" asked Ginger, who did not quite understand how anybody could wish for anything else but a banana.

"I did not wish for anything," Froger explained. "I just told everybody what the magic chant was."

"Swish-swish! I wish! For a banana!" Ginger pleaded and looked expectantly at the tree: "Where is it?"

"Ginger, you shouldn't be so careless with magic chants," Maggie warned her. "You might get bananas growing out of your ears."

"I don't care where they grow from! I just really want one!"

"If you hurry, you won't get anything," Froger warned her. "You have to be patient."

"Patient with magic?"

"Especially with magic! Sit down for a moment, let me try."

Ginger sat down reluctantly. "I bet you he will wish for chocolates or some cake now," she grumbled.

"Everybody, close your eyes!" Froger said. He sat cross-legged, his cape fluttering behind his back like a big shiny wing. He then pressed his supple hands to his temples and rocked gently from side to side chanting:

The magic wind goes swash and swish,
The apple tree grows what I wish!
I don't want chocolate or cakes,
Just grow the cookies Maggie bakes!

A slight purple breeze, so delicate, you could hardly feel it, touched the apple tree. Everybody opened their eyes and gasped. Swaying serenely on the tree's branches were Maggie's tasty cookies! Gregg pulled off his glasses.

"It is impossible!" he proclaimed and was the first one to dash to the tree and pick one cookie.

"Tastes just like Maggie's!" he announced and, without skipping a beat, reached for another one. While everybody was enjoying Froger's delicious dream, Ginger ran in circles around the tree panting heavily:

Swash! Swish!
For banana I wish!

"Have a cookie," Mrs.Cluck offered, but by the time Ginger stopped running, all of the cookies were gone.

"It's not working!" Ginger complained and leaned against the apple tree trying to catch her breath.

"Oh, I know what I shall wish for!" Ferret said. He sat down just like Froger, held onto the tips of his bandanna, and chanted slowly:

The magic wind goes swash and swish,
The apple tree grows what I wish!

Try really hard, don't hurry, please,
And give us some delicious cheese!

And again, a subtle breeze went through the tree's branches, leaving behind a light cloud. When everybody opened their eyes, little pieces of cheese wrapped in silver foils were hanging from the twigs.

"It worked!" Ferret cried. "Everybody, help yourselves!"

"Oh, look at this!" Ginger moaned. "All these cookies and cheeses and not a single banana!"

"It's so good!" Maggie called, "Ginger, you should have some!"

But Ginger was busy jumping up high and yelling at the top of her lungs:

No more cookies, no more cheese!
Just one banana, please, please, please!
Swash! Swish! I wish!

"What's going on? Why isn't my banana showing up?"

"Maybe you are trying too hard, Ginger," Maggie said. "Let me see how it works." And she closed her eyes and sang softly:

The magic wind goes swash and swish,
The apple tree grows what I wish!
I'm telling you about my dream:
Could you please give us some ice cream!

"It worked again!" Ginger cried when she opened her eyes. "What am I doing wrong?" And while everybody feasted on ice cream in tiny cones and sugar cups, she chanted with all her might:

Will it hurt you swashy-swish!
A banana is my wish!

"Why don't you wish slowly?" Mrs. Cluck suggested. "You are wishing too fast! Look!" Mrs. Cluck closed her eyes:

The magic wind goes swash and swish,
The apple tree grows what I wish!
Could we all here please be fed
Some piping hot, delicious bread!

The scrumptious smell of freshly baked breads reached everybody's noses so fast, they were all drooling as they ran up to the tree to take down hot crusty buns.

"This is impossible!" Ginger got very upset now. She was hungry because she never had a chance to taste anything and tired from wishing for her banana so hard. "I am not playing this game anymore! I'm out!"

"Come on, Ginger," coaxed her Gregg, who had to admit he was enjoying the whole experience more than he ever thought he would. "You just have to concentrate!"

The magic wind goes swash and swish,
The apple tree grows what I wish!
And now for everybody's sake
Could we please have some chocolate cake?

Ginger turned away and didn't even look how everybody reached for the chocolate cupcakes hanging from the tree and how their fingers and faces got covered with the rich chocolate frosting.

"So good!" Gregg giggled and swallowed the last piece of his wish. Mrs. Cluck eyed her son with surprise because she had never heard him giggle before.

"Our turn! Our turn!" Tip and Top cried. They closed their eyes and chanted together:

The magic wind goes swash and swish,
The apple tree grows what we wish!
Of all the most delicious eats
Could we please all get yummy sweets?

"Even babies know how to do it!"
Ginger groaned, lying on the ground
and looking at the tree in despair.
The candies fluttered
happily in the branches
sparkling in their gold
and silver wraps.

"We will all have a
sugar shock!" Denny cried, sucking
on a cherry lollipop. "We have to try something
different!" And he sang:

The magic wind goes swash and swish,
The apple tree grows what I wish!
It would be nice if we could try
A little bit of pizza pie!

Unbelievable! Even Gregg would have admitted–if he had time to, of course–that though cakes and cookies growing on an apple tree were an outstanding sight, slices of pizza hanging from the tree's branches were beyond anybody's imagination! But there they were, hot and dripping with cheese, begging for everybody to take a bite out of them.

"Please, can I have the pepperoni!" Ferret cried. "And the double cheese!"

Ginger couldn't stand it any longer.

"How could that be?" she burst out crying, and angry tears sprayed out of her eyes. "Everybody got something, but I dreamed first and got nothing! Nothing!" she sobbed.

Ginger gets her wish

"Ginger, don't cry!" Maggie ran up to the monkey and hugged her.

"I want my banana!" she wailed. "Just one little, scrawny yellow banana!"

"I know what we should do," Maggie said. "Let's all wish for Ginger!"
They all sat down in a circle and held hands.

The magic wind goes swash and swish,
The apple tree grows what we wish!
And let us see a long liana
With Ginger's favorite banana!

"At last!!!" Ginger cried as she opened her eyes and ran up to the tree. "My banana! My! My!" and she kissed the yellow fruit and then– without even offering any to her friends, not a single little bite–she swallowed it whole!

"You have to peel it first!" Gregg warned her, but it was too late.

Ginger first smiled happily and then started waving her arms very fast and making funny sounds.

"Ginger is so happy she wants to fly!" guessed Tip.

"Ginger is so happy she is dancing!" guessed Top.
But they both guessed wrong!

"Ginger is suffocating!" Gregg cried.

"What is that?" asked Tip and Top.

"The banana got stuck in her throat, and she cannot breathe!" Gregg explained, while Denny quickly ran up to Ginger and hugged her firmly from behind, clasping his hands right under her chest.

"Heimlich maneuver!" he cried and suddenly squeezed Ginger tightly with his arms.

Squawk! The banana popped out of Ginger's throat, flew high into the air,

and struck Froger's head, knocking him out.

"Agh!" Froger wailed and conveniently fell again right into Maggie's arms.

"Swish, swish!" Ferret slapped him.

"What are you doing?" Froger cried. "Don't you see I'm unconscious?!"

"Huggy-buggy! Not anymore!" Ferret grinned and helped Maggie sit Froger up on the ground.

Ginger was breathing in and out slowly, filling her chest with fresh air.

"That was such a wonderful manure!" Mrs. Cluck said to Denny. "I have never seen any like that!"

"It was 'maneuver', Mother, not 'manure'! Maneuver is a special move!" Gregg corrected her.

"Why did Denny say he had ham locked in it?" Tip and Top wondered.

"Nobody locked any ham anywhere," Gregg said with importance. "The only thing locked was the banana in Ginger's throat. Denny squeezed her tight, and it came out—it's called Heim-lich man-eu-ver. Heimlich was the doctor who invented it."

"I was very impressed," Ferret said. "You are a doctor yourself, Denny!"

"I was impressed even more," Froger said, rubbing the banana's impression on his forehead, which started forming into bump. "I thought I was hit by a torpedo!"

"I am sorry," Ginger whispered. "I got greedy . . . I didn't even share with anybody . . . Is that banana still good to eat?" she asked miserably.

"No, Ginger, I wouldn't eat it," Maggie said. "We'll try and get you a banana some other time. I think Froger has saved some cookies. Maybe he will share with you."

"Oh, all right," Froger said reluctantly. "They're almost like Maggie's, but Maggie's are still better."

"Thank you, Froger," Ginger said and bit hungrily into the treat. "I almost killed you, and you are sharing your favorite food with me!"

"That's what friends are for," Froger said kindly.

"I'll bake more for you," Maggie promised as she helped Froger up. He leaned happily on Maggie's arm and walked a little wobbly by her side—he was a wounded soldier after all!

"Huggy-buggy!" Ferret mocked him, wiped his mouth with his bandanna, and started digging a new tunnel.

When everybody left, Ginger came up to Ferret's hole and called him.

"Ferret, could I please borrow one of your broken shovels?"

"All right, but don't break it any further!" Ferret got out of his hole and handed one to Ginger.

"I'll be very careful with it!" she promised. She looked around and found the sunniest spot in the yard. She dug a small hole there, put her banana in it, and covered it with some dirt.

"That should work," she said. "Imagine how surprised everybody will be next year when they see the biggest banana tree in the world with heaps of bananas on it? I'll share with everybody! I promise!"

The apple tree heard her, and its leaves rustled softly in the gentle purple breeze. Summer was just around the corner with new adventures to come.